TIME TWISTERS

ABRAHAM LINCOLN PRO WRESTLER

ALSO BY STEVE SHEINKIN

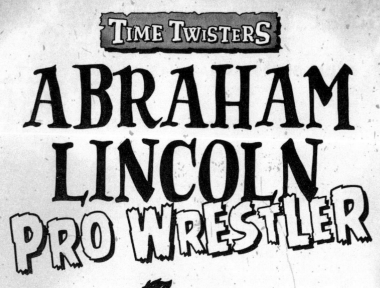

TIME TWISTERS

ABRAHAM LINCOLN

PRO WRESTLER

STEVE SHEINKIN

ILLUSTRATED BY NEIL SWAAB

ROARING BROOK PRESS

New York

Text copyright © 2018 by Steve Sheinkin

Illustrations copyright © 2018 by Neil Swaab

Published by Roaring Brook Press

Roaring Brook Press is a division of Holtzbrinck Publishing Holdings Limited Partnership

175 Fifth Avenue, New York, NY 10010

mackids.com

Library of Congress Cataloging-in-Publication Data

Names: Sheinkin, Steve, author. | Swaab, Neil, illustrator.

Title: Abraham Lincoln, pro wrestler / Steve Sheinkin ; Illustrated by Neil Swaab.

Description: First edition. | New York : Roaring Brook Press, 2018. | Series: Time Twisters |
  Summary: Abby and her stepbrother, Doc, must persuade Abraham Lincoln to play his part in
  history after one too many comments about history being boring cause him to go on strike. |

Identifiers: LCCN 2017005891 (print) | ISBN 9781250148919 (hardcover)

Subjects: LCSH: Lincoln, Abraham, 1809–1865—Juvenile fiction. | CYAC: Lincoln, Abraham,
  1809-1865—Fiction. | History—Fiction. | Schools—Fiction. | Stepfamilies—Fiction.

Classification: LCC PZ7.1.S512 (ebook) | LCC PZ7.1.S512 Abr 2018 (print) | DDC [Fic]—dc23

LC record available at https://lccn.loc.gov/2017005891

Our books may be purchased in bulk for promotional, educational, or business use. Please contact
your local bookseller or the Macmillan Corporate and Premium Sales Department at (800) 221-7945
ext. 5442 or by e-mail at MacmillanSpecialMarkets@macmillan.com.

First edition, 2018

Book design by Neil Swaab

Printed in the United States of America by LSC Communications, Harrisonburg, Virginia

1   3   5   7   9   10   8   6   4   2

For Braiden White's second-grade class at Division Street Elementary—thanks for all the great ideas!

ABRAHAM LINCOLN
PRO WRESTLER

CHAPTER ONE

Ms. Maybee said, "Okay, guys, let's get out our history books!"

The whole class groaned.

Doc tilted his head back and started snoring.

"Very funny," Ms. Maybee said. "This is going to be fun, trust me. Abby? How about if you get us started."

Abby—she's the one who broke history. It was Abby and her stepbrother, Doc.

You can thank them later.

ABBY

DOC

ZZZZZZZ

Everyone took out their textbooks. Thick books. Heavy. Kids lifted them high and let them drop onto their desks. It sounded like thunder.

Ms. Maybee just shook her head.

"Page one twenty-five," she said. "Today we'll read about Abraham Lincoln."

More groans. And Doc sang out, "Bor—ing!"

Ms. Maybee glared at the class. "Who said that?"

Everyone knew. But no one said.

"Well, whoever it was," Ms. Maybee said, looking right at Doc, "you should be aware that you are not only rude, but also totally wrong."

She pointed to a poster of Abraham Lincoln taped to the classroom wall.

Best. President. Ever.

HONEST ABE

4

"Abraham Lincoln is one of our most important presidents," she said. "He basically saved the country and ended slavery. And he's certainly *not* boring. Come on, you'll see." And she said, "Abby, when you're ready."

Abby opened the textbook to page 125. There was an old black-and-white picture of a house with a horse and wagon driving by. She read what it said at the top of the page: "Lincoln: from Lawyer to President."

"A little louder, Abby," Ms. Maybee said. "We're going to show these people how exciting history can be!"

She read louder: "Abraham Lincoln sat at a large desk in his office in the city of Springfield, Illinois. He was reading a newspaper. After a little while, he put the newspaper down and stood up. He walked out of the room. He came back carrying a cup of coffee. He sat down again. He picked up the newspaper and began to read."

Abby looked up from the book, pretty confused.

"See," Doc said. "Nap time."

For once, Ms. Maybee didn't yell at him. "Okay," she said, "that wasn't the most thrilling part, I'll admit. Doc, since you're so interested, why don't you see what comes next?"

He read aloud: "Abraham Lincoln turned to the next page of the newspaper. He took a sip of coffee. He put his feet up on his desk. He read some more. Every few minutes he sipped his drink."

Doc stopped. "Do I have to keep going?" he asked.

"No, that's fine," Ms. Maybee said.

She looked at her own copy of the textbook. "According to what it says here, he just sat at his desk all day. He read the paper, drank coffee, and, um, that's it. That's all he did."

"Why do we have to know this stuff?" Doc asked.

"It's important," Ms. Maybee said.

"Why?"

"It just is," she said. "Hmmm . . ." She was still looking at her book. "This really doesn't seem right. I remember Lincoln *doing* a lot more. But to be totally honest, history was never my favorite subject."

"Because it's boring!" Doc said.

"Well, this book is a little dry, I'll admit," Ms. Maybee said.

She closed the textbook and said, "Let's do a math worksheet."

And a few kids actually cheered.

CHAPTER TWO

When the school day ended, Abby walked through the library to the storage room in the back. It was a small room packed with books—books on shelves, in cardboard boxes, and stacked up on the floor. There were two chairs and a table and one small window.

Abby sat and started taking stuff out of her backpack.

Another boring afternoon . . .

This happened every day. Abby and Doc's mother was a teacher at the school and ran an after-school program for younger kids. Their dad taught at the middle school and stayed late to coach track. So every day, after school, Abby and Doc had to stick around for about an hour, until their mom was ready to leave. They were supposed to sit in this room and do homework or read.

It was usually the longest hour of the day. Not this time.

Doc came in and tossed down his backpack. He stepped onto a chair, then onto the table, and from there he climbed onto one of the stacks of boxes. His head almost touched the ceiling.

Think I could jump from here to that big box?

He pointed to a tall box about six feet away.

"Probably," Abby said. "But I'm not saying you'd live."

"I'm the Amazing, um, no, I'm Doctor Frog-Leg!"

"You are?"

"Well, that's my pro-wrestling name," he said.

That was the big thing in school that week. There was going to be a pro-wrestling tournament in the gym Friday night, and kids were joking about what their wrestler names would be.

"Watch this!" Doc said.

Abby looked down at her notebook. Her mom had married Doc's dad three years before, so she was used to him. They mostly got along. But sometimes she felt it was best to ignore him.

For example, any time he said "Watch this!"

"I'm really gonna do it," he said.

"I'm trying to read," she said.

"Here goes!" he said.

"Hold on!" a voice shouted. "Don't jump on me!"

Doc looked at Abby.

"That wasn't me," she said.

"Don't jump!" the voice said again. A man's voice.

Abby pointed to the big box. "Almost sounds like it was coming from . . ."

The box shook. Something was moving around inside it.

The voice said, "It's so dark in here." The box flaps flipped open, and the voice said, "Ah, that's better."

Then a black hat appeared, then a head, then a chest. It was a tall man in a black suit. He had a thin, bony face and wild hair sticking out from under his hat.

He looked a lot like Abraham Lincoln.

CHAPTER THREE

Abby stood so fast her chair fell over.

Doc was frozen in pre-jump position, knees bent and arms out in front of him.

The man in the box lifted a very long leg and tried to step out, but the whole thing tipped over. He tumbled to the floor with a loud thud. His tall hat went flying and a few pieces of paper fell out.

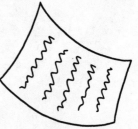

Slowly, calmly, like nothing unusual was going on, the man collected the papers. He stuck them in the lining of his hat. He stood and dusted off his jacket.

The guy really looked exactly like the poster of

Abraham Lincoln in their classroom. Except he didn't have that beard-but-no-mustache you always see in Lincoln pictures.

He said, "How many legs does a dog have, if you call the tail a leg?"

Abby was too stunned to speak.

Doc said, "Um, five?"

"No, only four," the man said, smiling. "Calling the tail a leg doesn't make it a leg!" He roared with laughter.

He was the only one.

"I see you don't care for my jokes," the man said. "Well, you're in good company. Mrs. Lincoln is very much on your side." And he laughed again.

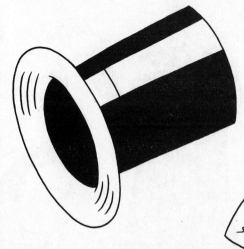

"Forgive me for dropping in like this. I'm Abraham Lincoln."

He held out his right hand to Abby. They shook.

"Abby," she said. "That's Doc."

The visitor reached up and shook hands with Doc.

"Pleasure to meet you, friend," he said. "Need help getting down?"

"Not really," Doc said. "But since you're standing right there." He rested a hand on the man's shoulder and jumped to the ground.

The man looked around.

He was still acting like everything was normal.

"So, um," Abby said. "Who actually are you?"

He laughed. "I'm truly Abraham Lincoln, I assure you."

"Then where's your beard?" Doc asked. "Everyone knows you have a beard."

"Oh, I grew that later. It's a good story, actually."

The man claiming to be Lincoln sat down and folded one leg over the other. The look on his face turned serious.

"But we have more important matters to discuss than facial hair," he said. "I want to talk to you about what happened today. In class, when you were reading the history book, you may have noticed that the story didn't seem quite right."

"You mean the part where Lincoln just sat at his desk?" Doc said.

"And read a newspaper?" Abby added.

"Lovely way to spend the day," the man said. "But all wrong! Don't you see?"

They didn't see.

"It's not what's supposed to happen!" the man shouted. "And that's all your fault!"

"Ours?" Abby asked.

"Yes, yours. Both of you, your class, your teacher . . ."

Abby and Doc both started to think of a lot of questions. But the man didn't give them time to ask.

"We can hear what you say, you know," he said. "When you say, 'History is boring.' When you make snoring noises."

"Wasn't me," Doc said.

"Please, friend," the man said. "We hear it all. How do you think that makes us feel?"

"Hold on," Abby said. "You're saying 'we' . . . you mean you and, um . . ."

"I mean myself, yes. And all the other

people from history. Everyone. We hear everything you say."

Yes, we're looking at **YOU**.

The box he'd come out of was still on its side. Abby bent down to look in. There were a few books in the back corner.

"How did you get here?" she asked.

"What matters is that I'm here," he said. "Just this once. I'm here to tell you that I won't stand for it anymore."

"Stand for what?" Doc asked.

"Snoring, for one thing," the man said, looking right into Doc's eyes. "Saying I'm boring, groaning in agony when it comes time to read about history. As I said, today was just a warning. If you do it again—well, you'll see."

He set the box upright.

"And believe me, you won't like it," he said. "Now, help me get back into this thing."

Doc and Abby held the box steady. The tall man stood on a chair, leaned forward, and sort of stepped, sort of belly flopped into the box.

But with no sound.

Abby stood on her tiptoes to look into the box. It was about as tall as she was. And empty, except for the books at the bottom.

CHAPTER FOUR

The next morning, as always, Doc and Abby got to school early with their mom. She went right to her classroom, and Doc and Abby walked to the cafeteria for breakfast.

"So should we say something?" Abby asked.

"You mean about Lincoln?"

"Yeah," Abby said. "About what he said. Warn the class or something?"

"Like what?" Doc said. "Like, 'Oh, hi, class, I just wanted to let you know that yesterday, after school, Abraham Lincoln appeared in a cardboard box and told me and Abby to tell you guys not to make fun of history.'"

"That does sound kind of weird."

They slid their trays toward the cash register. Mr. Biddle, the gym teacher, was ahead of them in line.

"Morning, guys," he said.

"Good morning, Mr. Biddle," they both said.

They carried their food to a table and started to eat.

"Anyway, there's no way it was *really* Lincoln," Doc said with a mouthful of toast. "I mean, he lived in the eighteen, you know, somethings."

"So who do you think it was?"

"I don't know," Doc said. He looked at Mr. Biddle, who was standing nearby, joking around with a few kids. "Maybe it was *him*."

"Mr. Biddle?" Abby asked.

"Looked sort of like him."

"A tiny bit," Abby said. "But why would he do that? He mostly likes dodgeball. And how did he just disappear into the box like that?"

Doc sipped his chocolate milk. "Couldn't tell you."

———————

"Okay, you lucky ducks," Ms. Maybee told the class later that morning. "It's that time again. That special time you've all been waiting for, hoping for, praying for . . ."

Abby turned and looked at Doc.

"That's right," chirped Ms. Maybee. "Time to get out those history textbooks!"

Groans, grumbles, sighs, snores.

Abby looked up at the picture of Abe Lincoln on the wall. He seemed to be staring right at her.

But what could she do?

Ms. Maybee laughed. "You big babies, today's going to be better. We'll read about how Lincoln became president of the United

States and faced the Civil War, the greatest crisis in American history."

Then came the usual cracks:

"Do we have to?"

"Can't we just watch glue dry instead?"

"Let's do another math worksheet!"

Everyone was laughing—except Abby, Doc, and the teacher. Normally Doc would have jumped in with a joke of his own. Everyone was expecting him to.

Instead, he said, "Let's give it a chance."

The other kids were in shock.

"I like history," Doc said.

"No you don't!" someone shouted.

"Well," Doc said, "it could be, you know, not too terrible."

"Thank you, Doc," Ms. Maybee said. "Louis, get us started. Page one twenty-six."

Louis read out loud: "Abraham Lincoln sat in a rocking chair in the living room of his house. He was wearing a robe and slippers. He was reading a newspaper."

Louis looked up from the book. "It's the same as yesterday. He's not doing anything."

Ms. Maybee looked worried. But she said, "Keep going, please."

"Lincoln sat in the chair, reading, for about an hour. Then he got up. He folded the newspaper and tucked it under his arm. He walked out the back door to a tiny white building behind the house. It was the family outhouse, a  three-holer. Lincoln opened the door and—"

"Okay, let's stop there," Ms. Maybee cut in. She looked down at her own copy of the book and read a little more. "Oh, *gross*," she said.

And she shut the book. History was over for the day.

Possibly forever.

CHAPTER FIVE

After school, in the storage room behind the library, Abby dragged a chair over to the big box—Lincoln's box. She stood on the chair, opened the top flaps of the box, and looked in.

Nothing down there but the textbooks.

"He's not coming back," Doc said from the doorway. He came in and shut the door behind him. "He said he'd give us just one chance."

"So what are we supposed to do?"

"Nothing."

"That's it, then?" Abby asked. "Lincoln's just going to sit there forever?"

"Looks like it," Doc said.

He jumped onto the table, then onto the wobbly stack of boxes he'd climbed the day before. "I never did get to make that jump."

"It's all our fault," Abby said. "He warned us."

"Hey, I tried," Doc said. "You didn't. Think I can make it? To the big box?"

Abby rolled her eyes. "Don't be stupid," she said. "The box is almost empty."

"So?"

"So you'll fall right through and break your—ugh, who cares."

"Watch this!"

Abby sat down at the table and opened her backpack.

Doc said, "I'm really going to!"

Abby took out a book and started reading.

Doc screamed,

YAAAAAAAHHHH!

as he jumped. He sailed across the room, made it to the big box, hit the top flaps of the box feet-first, fell through, and disappeared.

No crashing sound. No screams of pain.

Abby waited. The box didn't move.

She got up and stood on her tiptoes and looked in.

On the bottom was the layer of books. Nothing else.

———•———

Doc came down hard in a cloud of dust.

"Look out, there!" a man shouted.

Doc looked up. A horse-drawn wagon was rattling right toward him.

Doc froze. The wagon swerved and the wheels of the wagon missed Doc's legs by inches.

"Get out of the road!" the driver yelled.

Road? Doc wondered. What road? Doc looked around. Yep, he was on the road. A wide, dirt road. And another wagon was heading his way.

He bounced to his feet and ran to the sidewalk. He was standing there, brushing

the dust off his jeans, when Abby landed a few yards away.

"Over here!" Doc shouted to her.

She dodged a galloping horse and made it to the sidewalk.

He was smiling at her. "You jumped."

"Into the box? Yeah."

"I'm proud of you," Doc said.

"For being as dumb as you?"

"As daring, you mean."

"Okay, fine," Abby said.

"Where are we?"

"Not a clue," he said.

They looked around. Horses and carriages rolled down the dirt road. People walked by on the sidewalk—men in old-fashioned suits, women in dresses. Two- and three-story brick buildings lined the road.

"It's like history," Doc said. "Except, you know, in color."

Abby stepped in front of a woman who was passing by.

"Hi, sorry," Abby said. "Silly question, but . . . remind me of where we are?"

"Pardon me, child?"

"Like, the name of this town. What is it again?"

The woman looked Abby up and down, then Doc. "This is Springfield, Illinois," she said. "Where did you get those strange clothes?"

"I think the mall," Doc said.

"And what year is it?" asked Abby.

But the woman was already hurrying away. Looking slightly scared.

Abby and Doc started walking in the other direction.

"So what do you think?" Doc asked. "We're inside a book?"

"Or back in time?" Abby wondered. "Like *The Magic Treehouse*?"

"*The Magic Cardboard Box*," Doc said. "That doesn't sound as good."

"No, it doesn't. Maybe it's a dream?"

"Must be your dream, then. Mine are more exciting."

They crossed the street and walked down a block with wooden houses.

"You know, zooming over cities, fighting zombies," Doc said. "Either that or I go to school in my underwear."

"Thanks for sharing," Abby said. "Hey, that looks like the picture in our textbook."

She pointed to a house on the corner of Eighth and Jackson Streets. It was a light brown two-story house with green shutters.

"Lincoln's house?" Doc said.

"I think so," Abby said. "What are those kids doing?"

Four kids were on the sidewalk in front of the house. One boy was sitting on another boy's shoulders. He was tying a string around a tree, as high up as he could reach.

"Hurry!" a third boy called from below.

The boy got the string tied. Then, still on his friend's shoulders, he pulled the other end of the string tight, so that it stretched across the sidewalk, about seven feet above the ground. The other kids crouched down, giggling.

Doc and Abby watched from across the street. The front door of the light brown house opened. The man who'd visited them the day before stepped out.

He really *was* Abraham Lincoln, and by now Doc and Abby believed it.

Lincoln walked down his porch steps, lost in thought. He turned onto the sidewalk—and headed right for the string.

CHAPTER SIX

He never saw it coming.

The top of Lincoln's tall black hat hit the string and flew off. Papers shot out and danced in the breeze. As Lincoln bent to gather the notes, the kids leaped onto his back and rode him like cowboys, laughing and shouting.

Abby and Doc couldn't believe it—

Lincoln didn't seem mad. Actually, he was laughing, too.

The kids jumped off Lincoln's back and ran down the street.

Lincoln scrambled after his last few papers. One blew across the street, toward Doc's feet. Doc bent to pick it up.

"Ah, it's you," Lincoln said, walking toward Doc and Abby. "They do that all the time, those boys. You'd think I wouldn't keep falling for it."

Doc handed Lincoln the piece of paper.

"Thank you," Lincoln said. "Nice of you to come, but it's all over. I'm all done."

"With what?" asked Abby.

"With history," Lincoln said. "I did warn you, after all. And now it's final. You thought history was boring before? *Now* I'll show you boring!"

"You mean you're quitting?" Abby asked. "Quitting history?"

"Yes, exactly," Lincoln said. "I can't speak for other people—Pocahontas, George Washington, Harriet Tubman. Though I know they're angry, too. As I said, we hear you. And since you insist on saying our lives are boring, well then, we'll show you. You can read about us sitting in chairs, staring at the wall. See how you like it."

"But don't you do really important things?" Doc asked.

"Not anymore," Lincoln said. "As of now, I'm on vacation."

"Mr. Lincoln! Look at you!"

A woman in a long dress strode up. She was just over five feet tall, with blue eyes and brown hair pulled back in a bun. Doc and Abby recognized her from pictures they'd seen—Mary Lincoln, Abe's wife.

"You're covered in dust," she said, brushing off her husband's jacket.

She barely came up to his chest. He put

a hand on her shoulder, turned to Doc and Abby, and said, "I'm Abraham, and she's Mary. That's the *long* and the *short* of it."

And he burst into loud, high-pitched laughter.

Abby and Doc just stood there.

"You tell such *old* jokes, Mr. Lincoln," Mary said.

"Well, I'm an old man!" Abe said, laughing again. But he didn't look that old, not when he smiled. "Now," he said, "if you'll excuse me."

And Lincoln walked toward the center of town.

"I don't suppose he's going to work," Mary said.

"No," Doc said. "He said he was quitting."

"Forever," Abby said. "No more history."

Mary groaned. "The election is tomorrow!"

"What if he doesn't become president?" Abby asked.

"Then we're doomed!" Mrs. Lincoln wailed. "The country will break apart! Everything we have worked for—all thrown away!"

She spun, ran to her house, went in, and slammed the door behind her.

"She seemed upset," Doc said.

"Well, we broke history," Abby said. "That's sort of a big deal."

They started walking.

"Abe Lincoln's not how I expected," Doc said.

"I know," Abby said. "I kind of like him."

"I know. And the funny thing is, I want to know what he's going to do. In history, I mean."

"Me too."

"Also, saving the country would be good," Doc said.

"We have to find him," Abby said.

"Let's go!"

They took off running.

CHAPTER SEVEN

Doc and Abby sprinted into town, along busy streets.

No sign of Lincoln.

They saw a brick building with a sign above the door that said: LINCOLN-HERNDON LAW OFFICES. They ran up and looked through the window.

They ran another block, skidding to a stop in front of an alley between two buildings.

Lincoln was in the alley, hitting a small ball against the brick wall with his hand. The ball hit the wall, bounced, and Lincoln hit it again.

"I used to do this to relax," Lincoln said when he noticed Doc and Abby watching. "Back when I had a stressful job. What can I do for you?"

"Come meet our class!" Doc shouted.

"Excuse me?"

"Tomorrow," Abby said. "Come to our school and talk to our class."

"And they'll see that you're actually a pretty cool guy!" Doc added.

Lincoln caught the ball and turned toward them.

"Please," Abby said. "They'll love you, I know it!"

"They really will," Doc agreed. "And then you can go back to doing, you know . . . all your history stuff."

"History stuff," Lincoln said. "Like what?"

"You know, *stuff*," Doc said. "Being such a great president, signing the thing, the . . . Declaration of Independence?"

Lincoln put his hand on Doc's shoulder.

My young friend. You don't seriously think I signed the Declaration of Independence.

Um . . .

"From now on, we'll pay attention," Abby promised. "The whole class will, once they get to know you a little."

Lincoln's mouth stayed stiff. But his eyes were shining.

"You know where to find us," Doc said. "Oh, yeah, and one more thing."

"Yes?"

"How do we get out of here?"

Lincoln leaned down to them and spoke quietly. "You won't tell anyone?"

They shook their heads.

Lincoln said, "You have to close your eyes."

They did.

"And flap your arms like an eagle."

They did.

"And shout, 'We love history!'"

They shouted, "We love history!"

"Louder!"

"We love history!"

But nothing happened. Except that a guy riding by on a horse looked over and said, "Thank you!"

Doc and Abby stopped flapping their arms. They opened their eyes. They were still in the alley.

"Forgive me," Lincoln said, laughing. "I couldn't resist."

"Mary's right," Abby said. "There's such a thing as too many jokes."

"I know, I know," Lincoln said. And he started to look a little worried.

"What?" Abby asked.

"The truth is," Lincoln said, "I don't know how *you* leave."

"How did *you* get to *us*?" Abby asked.

"I'm not supposed to say."

"Please," Doc said. "It's our only chance to help you. Pretty much all the kids in our class think history is boring—"

At that instant, they disappeared.

And reappeared in the cardboard box in the storage room behind the library.

CHAPTER EIGHT

That night, after dinner, Abby and her dad were sitting on the couch in their living room. He was grading homework for his social studies class.

The TV was on, and Abby was changing channels, looking for something to watch.

Next on *Catching Up with the Carlisles* . . . Got you now, punk . . . Ha! Ha! Ha! . . . Act now before . . . Back to *Antiquity Bros* . . .

"Hey, stop!" Mr. Douglass said, looking up from his work. "A history show!"

Abby started to complain—but stopped herself.

"Great," she said. "I like history."

The screen showed a photo of an old house. A house Abby recognized.

"That's Springfield, Illinois," she said. "Abraham and Mary Lincoln's house!"

Her dad was impressed. "How'd you know that?"

"Let's just watch," Abby said.

The narrator of the show was saying: "The Lincoln home in Springfield was normally a lively place, with friends and political allies coming and going at all hours. But in the fall of 1860, when Abraham Lincoln was a candidate for president of the United States, the house was unusually quiet."

The TV showed a photo of the inside of the house. Lincoln was sitting in a chair.

"Lincoln refused to talk about the coming election," the narrator said. "In fact, he did not do anything at all. He just sat in a rocking chair, reading. All day. Every day. That's it. Well, sometimes, he played handball in an alley near his office. But really, not much else."

53

Lincoln's waiting, Abby thought. *Waiting to see what happens at our school tomorrow.*

"Terrible show," Mr. Douglass said. "Put on the basketball game."

Abby flipped to the game. "Dad," she said, "what's the big deal about history?"

"I'd be out of a job without it."

Abby hadn't thought of that.

Doc walked in from the kitchen with a bag of chips. "She means, why do we have to know it?"

"You don't *have* to," Mr. Douglass said. "That's just something we tell kids. But knowing history makes you smarter, helps you understand the world better. Mostly, it's just fun."

"Kids say it's . . ." Abby lowered her voice to a whisper, "boring."

"Some shows are boring, some books," Mr. Douglass said. "But history is just stories. Surprising, sad, funny, gross stories. Set in all different times and places. What's boring about that? Haven't you read about Lincoln in school?"

"Not so much," Abby said.

Mr. Douglass smiled. He loved any excuse to talk about history. "Well, Lincoln ran for president in 1860, right? The country was bitterly divided, mainly over the issue of slavery. About four million African Americans were living in slavery in the Southern states."

THE U.S.A. IN 1860

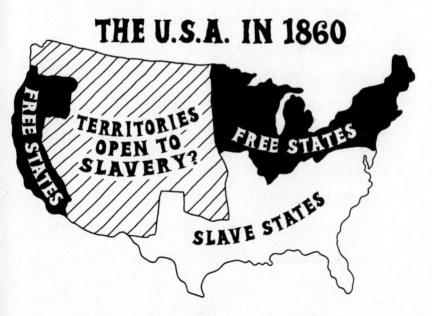

FREE STATES

TERRITORIES OPEN TO SLAVERY?

FREE STATES

SLAVE STATES

"And Lincoln was against slavery?" Doc asked.

"He knew it was wrong," Mr. Douglass said. "But he thought it would take a long time to get rid of it. His goal was to stop slavery from spreading to new states. Most of what's now the western United States hadn't been made into states yet. Should slavery be allowed there? Lincoln said no. Voters in the South said yes. Of course, enslaved people couldn't vote. Or women, either."

"What?" Abby asked. "Why not?"

"That was the law."

"That's not fair!"

"No," their dad said, "but listen."

"He's in teacher mode," Doc whispered. "There's no stopping him."

And there really wasn't.

"Lincoln won the election, but Southern leaders wouldn't accept him as president.

56

They chose to drop out of the United States and form their own government.

We'll call it the Confederate States of America!

"But Lincoln was ready to fight to hold the country together—that fight was the Civil War. Lincoln made mistakes, sure, like hiring some lousy generals. But he also did great things, like the Emancipation Proclamation—"

Doc slapped himself on the forehead.

"That's what I was trying to think of!" he said. "When we were talking with Lincoln today. I knew he signed something good."

Mr. Douglass turned to his son.

"So the Emancipation thing," Doc said. "What'd it do, again?"

"Proclamation," Mr. Douglass said. "It set the goal of freeing all enslaved people in the Confederate States. Up to this point, the Civil War had been about saving the Union. After the Emancipation Proclamation, the goal was to save the Union *and* end slavery. And let's not forget Lincoln's speeches, his beautiful dreams for our country!"

Mr. Douglass leaped from the couch, sending homework flying. "This nation, under God, shall have a new birth of freedom!" he roared. "And that government of the people, by the people, for the people, shall not perish from the earth!"

"Nice," Doc said.

"Gettysburg Address," Mr. Douglass said.

"Did he tell jokes?" Abby asked.

"Bad ones, I think," he said. "I'll find you guys a good Lincoln book."

But that could be a problem. How could there be a good book about a guy who just sits in a chair?

Doc and Abby looked at each other. They'd lived together long enough to read each other's minds. *We have one chance to persuade Lincoln to go back to work. One last chance.*

CHAPTER NINE

ALL VISITORS MUST CHECK IN AT FRONT DESK.

That's what the sign on the front door of the school said. Abby pointed it out to Doc as they walked in the next morning. They skipped breakfast, heading straight for the library. They hurried past Ms. Ventura, the librarian, who was sipping coffee at her desk.

They opened the door to the storage room. Abraham Lincoln was in there, sitting with his feet up on the table, reading.

"Ready when you are," he said.

Abby and Doc went in and shut the door behind them.

"Okay," Doc said, "what we think you should do is—wait, do you hear that?"

There were voices outside the door. Ms. Ventura and a teacher. The voices were getting closer. Ms. Ventura was saying, "Yes, I have a few extra copies in the storage room. Hold on a sec, I'll get one."

"She's coming!" Doc cried.

"Get in the box!" Abby said, tugging Lincoln's sleeve.

"Why?" he said. "I just got out of the box."

"You don't have the sticker!" Doc said.

"Sticker?"

"Guests have to check in," Abby said. "They're really strict about it. They'll kick you out!"

"Help me into the box!" Lincoln said.

But the voices were right outside the door.

"No time!"

Doc jumped onto the table and slid open the window. "Quick!"

Lincoln stepped onto the table and dove out the window.

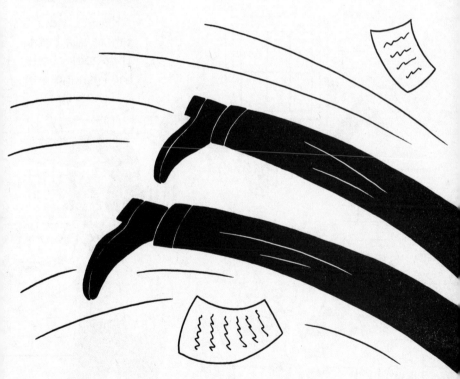

Or, he tried to. His hips got stuck in the window frame.

The door opened, and Ms. Ventura came in. "Excuse me," she said, "just need to grab something."

She turned toward a wall of shelves. She did not seem to notice that behind her, in the window, Abraham Lincoln was kicking his legs like an upside-down bug.

Hmm . . . now where did I put that book about the Pythagorean Theorem?

Doc reached for one of Lincoln's feet and gave it a shove. Lincoln slid out the window. There was a crashing sound.

"What was *that*?" Ms. Ventura asked, turning toward the noise.

"Soccer game," Doc said. He was still standing on the table. "Nice shot, Gomez!" he shouted out the window.

The librarian just shook her head. She'd given up trying to understand Doc. She tucked a book under her arm and said, "Well, I'll see you guys very soon."

"We don't have library today," Abby said.

"That's what you think," Ms. Ventura said. "Can't say more. It's a surprise!"

She smiled and left the room.

The top of Lincoln's hat was visible through the window. "Which way is the front door?" he asked.

"Hold on," Doc said. "We're coming."

A few minutes later, Mrs. Martin, the attendance clerk, looked up from her computer.

"Good morning, Abby, Doc," she said. Then she noticed a tall man standing next to them. "How may I help you?"

"Good morning to you, ma'am," Lincoln said. He tipped his hat. "My name is Abraham Lincoln."

"I can see that," Mrs. Martin said.

"He's here to visit our class today," Doc said. "We just need to get him one of those stickers guests have to wear."

"Of course," Mrs. Martin said. She tilted her head back to look up at Lincoln. "Very nice costume. No beard, though?"

"Beard?" Lincoln asked.

"You know," Mrs. Martin said, touching her chin.

"I'll grow it soon," Lincoln said. "I have come to meet with Doc and Abby's class. So if you will kindly give me the proper pass, we can be on our way."

Mrs. Martin was smiling. "He's not bad," she said to Doc.

Doc nodded. "We like him."

"But it would be better with the beard," she said. "You're an actor, I'm guessing?" she asked Lincoln.

"I'm a lawyer," he said.

"Makes sense," Mrs. Martin said. "Can't be much money in being an Abraham Lincoln, oh, what do they call it? Reenactor?"

"I also served one term in the United States Congress," Lincoln said.

"Good for you," Mrs. Martin said. "I'll just need to see a picture ID."

"Pardon?"

"Driver's license, please."

Lincoln looked at Abby and Doc.

"I don't have one," Lincoln said.

"How'd you get here?" Mrs. Martin asked.

"Hard to explain."

"How do you get around?" she asked Lincoln.

"Old Bob," he said.

"What?"

"That's my horse," Lincoln said. "His name is Old Bob."

"I see," Mrs. Martin said. "And what is *your* name?"

"Abraham Lincoln," Lincoln said. "No middle name."

Mrs. Martin wasn't smiling anymore.

Lincoln started to spell his name: "A-B-R-"

"I know how to spell it," Mrs. Martin cut him off.

"It sounds weird," Doc said. "But he really *is* Abraham Lincoln."

"Of course he is," Mrs. Martin said. "I still need a driver's license."

"Okay, fine, he's an actor," Abby said.

"And he's wearing a costume," Doc said. "That's why he doesn't have his wallet. He forgot it in his real clothes."

"Now *that* I believe," Mrs. Martin said.

"So he can go in?" Abby asked.

"Absolutely not."

Principal Darling stepped out of her office. She folded her arms across her chest and said,

CHAPTER TEN

"**S**o, to review," Doc said, "our plan to fix history: total failure."

"Check," Abby said.

After kicking Lincoln out of school, Principal Darling had sent Doc and Abby straight to their classroom. They were sitting at their desks. Class was about to start.

Abraham Lincoln was in the parking lot. Or somewhere out there.

After the usual morning announcements, Principal Darling reminded everyone about the wrestling tournament. "This is our big fundraiser for the year, and several famous wrestlers have agreed to donate their time. Can you believe that a man by the name of, I have it here somewhere, ah, yes, Gigantic Phil—"

Kids cheered. He was a pretty popular wrestler.

"—will be here in our very own gym tonight? It's going to be an exciting evening, and I hope to see you all there! Oh, and one more thing," she said. "All fourth-grade teachers and classes, please make your way to the library to meet a very special surprise guest. Have a great day, everyone."

"What's going on?" Doc asked.

Ms. Maybee was smiling. "You'll see," she said.

———•———

About a hundred kids crowded together on the library carpet in front of a Smart Board. The teachers sat in folding chairs behind the kids.

Ms. Maybee stood in front of the room with Ms. Ventura.

"We have a real treat for you," Ms. Maybee said. "A very special guest."

"That's right," Ms. Ventura said. "I've been hearing all about the history book you've been reading. How Abraham Lincoln just sits in his chair, doing nothing. But the real Lincoln is a lot more exciting. I can assure you—because I've just met him!"

Abby leaned toward Doc and whispered. "They must have let him in, after all."

"He's a clever guy," Doc said.

The librarian glared at them. They stopped talking.

"I know you'll show our guest respect by sitting quietly and raising your hand to ask questions," Ms. Ventura said. "Now, would you please welcome the greatest president of them all, Mr. Abraham Lincoln!"

Everyone clapped. Doc and Abby stood and cheered.

In walked a man in a black suit and a top hat. And a beard. He looked kind of like Abraham Lincoln.

But it was obviously Mr. Biddle, the gym teacher.

Doc and Abby sat down.

"Greetings, boys and girls!" Mr. Biddle called in a deep, booming voice—a voice that sounded nothing like Abraham Lincoln. "My name is Abraham Lincoln! And I am here to tell you about my life! How awesome is that?"

Kids laughed and hooted.

Mr. Biddle's beard was held on by a string that looped around his ears. A Chicago Cubs T-shirt was clearly visible under his white dress shirt.

A photo of a log cabin appeared on the Smart Board.

"Thanks, Jenny," Mr. Biddle said. "I mean Ms. Ventura. What marvelous technology you people have these days!"

He pointed to the screen. "As you may have heard, I was born in—" Mr. Biddle glanced at an index card in his hand. "In 1809, in Kentucky, making me the first president to be born outside the thirteen original states!

We lived in a log cabin with just one room and a dirt floor. Ever try sweeping a dirt floor? You sweep for an hour, and there's still dirt on the floor!"

That got some laughs.

"Next slide, please."

Ms. Ventura hit a button on her computer. The screen showed a drawing of a boy lying in front of a fireplace, reading.

"We moved to Indiana when I was about seven," Mr. Biddle said. "Farm chores kept me busy all day, but at night I would read by the light of the fire. It was my fondest wish to attend school, but the nearest schoolhouse was far away. So I got up before dawn each day and walked fifteen miles, through snowdrifts high above my head!"

"Come, now!" a voice called out. "Next you'll tell us it was uphill both ways!"

"I asked you to raise your hands," Ms. Ventura said.

But the comment had not come from one of the students. It had come from Abraham Lincoln.

The real one.

Time to drop some **actual** knowledge on you.

CHAPTER ELEVEN

Kids turned around to watch Abraham Lincoln walk through the library toward Mr. Biddle.

"This man is telling you one of those old Lincoln myths, walking fifteen miles to school," Lincoln said. "The truth is, I did not attend more than a year's worth of school in my entire—"

Lincoln tripped on the legs of seated kids and stumbled to the front of the room and crashed into the Smart Board.

"You all right, pal?" Mr. Biddle asked.

"Fine, thank you," Lincoln said, straightening his hat. "I am Abraham Lincoln."

"Me too," Mr. Biddle said.

They shook hands.

Lincoln turned to the kids and said, "But you see, I truly *am* Abraham Lincoln."

"You don't sound like him!" a kid shouted.

"Like who?" Lincoln asked.

"Like Lincoln," the kid said. "Your voice is too high." He pointed to Mr. Biddle. "He sounds more like Lincoln."

"Why, thank you, sir," Mr. Biddle said in his fake deep voice.

"How do you know what I sounded like?" Lincoln asked. "There are no recordings of my voice. I died about ten years before Thomas Edison invented the phonograph. The exact year of that invention slips my mind—which reminds me of a forgetful fellow I knew back in Illinois. One night he put his suit to bed and threw himself over the back of a chair!"

Lincoln laughed. No one else did.

"Good one," Abby said.

The room was silent.

"Um, does anyone mind if I continue?" asked Mr. Biddle.

"Please do," said Ms. Ventura.

The screen switched to a picture of young Lincoln chopping wood with an ax.

"I grew tall and strong in my teen years," Mr. Biddle said. "Look at those arms! You don't get pipes like that from sitting on the couch and playing video games!"

Mr. Biddle flexed like a bodybuilder. Kids laughed and cheered.

Who wants to feel the pythons?

Lincoln stepped in front of Mr. Biddle. "I was always eager to leave home," he said. "My father and I, we never did get along. So at nineteen, I took a job on a boat on the Mississippi River. I traveled all the way to New Orleans, which is where I saw slavery up close for the first time. Seeing that evil— human beings bought and sold—had a profound impact on my life."

Doc and Abby looked proud. Everyone else looked really confused.

Ms. Ventura said, "Who *is* this person?"

Doc jumped up and pointed to Lincoln. "He's really the real Abraham Lincoln!"

"It's true!" Abby said. "Ask him anything!"

"Where's your beard?" asked a boy up front.

"Beard, beard!" Lincoln moaned. "Does anyone care about anything but the beard?"

"It does seem a shame," Ms. Ventura said. "You've gone to the trouble of buying the whole Lincoln costume. Why not get the beard?"

"I've got the beard," Mr. Biddle said, rubbing his chin.

Lincoln took a deep breath. "Okay, the

beard story," he said. "When I was a candidate for president of the United States, I got a letter from a girl of eleven named Grace Bedell. Grace wrote that her father supported me, and that she was trying to persuade others to—well, I have the letter here somewhere."

He took off his hat and pulled out a folded piece of paper. He pointed to Maya, a girl sitting up front, saying, "Read this part here."

Maya stood, took the paper, and read:

If you let your whiskers grow, I will try and get the rest of them to vote for you. You would look a great deal better, for your face is so thin. All the ladies like whiskers and they would tease their husbands to vote for you and then you would be President.

The whole class laughed.

Doc and Abby smiled at each other. *The plan was working!*

"I was elected," Lincoln said, "and by February of 1861, when I set off for Washington, DC, I had the beard. My train stopped in many towns along the way, and I even met Grace Bedell in western New York, where she lived. I bent down to show her. . ."

Lincoln bent toward Maya, touched his chin, and said, "You see, I let these whiskers grow for you, Grace."

The class laughed again. Kids called out:

"That's hilarious!"

"What happened next?"

Lincoln smiled. "You really want to know?"

"Yeah!" lots of kids called.

"Forget history, let's talk about wrestling!" Mr. Biddle said. "How many of you guys are going to the big match tonight?"

"Wrestling?" Lincoln asked. "I've always

loved to wrestle. I'm even in the National Wrestling Hall of Fame!"

"No way," Mr. Biddle said.

"Honorary member," Lincoln said. "Look it up."

Turning to the kids, he said, "Back when I first moved to Illinois, there was this gang of town bullies. Everyone was afraid of them. But I challenged their leader, the toughest of the bunch, to a wrestling match. And I thrashed the man with the whole town looking on!"

That got a massive cheer.

"In this school, we prefer to use our words," Principal Darling said.

She was standing in the doorway, arms folded. She was glaring at Abraham Lincoln.

Doc said, "Uh-oh."

CHAPTER TWELVE

"**S**o, to review." Doc said, "Our plan to save history: complete disaster."

"Probably," Abby said. "Almost definitely."

It was after school. Doc and Abby were in the storage room. They hadn't seen Abraham Lincoln since Principal Darling threw him out of the school for the second time. They'd searched the parking lot and playground. No luck.

"Any chance he went back?" Doc said. "You know, to history?"

"One way to find out," Abby said.

She pulled a history textbook from the shelf and flipped to the section about Lincoln.

"Listen to this," she said, and read aloud: "November 6, 1860, was Election Day. It was perhaps the most important election in the nation's history. Abraham Lincoln, however, was missing. Mary Lincoln looked for her husband in his office in town. She checked the barbershop where he liked to talk with friends and the alley where he often played handball. He was nowhere to be found."

Abby closed the book.

"Yep," Doc said. "Disaster."

Abby was putting the book back on the shelf when the door flew open. Abraham Lincoln darted in and kicked the door shut. He bent over, hands on knees.

"I—" *pant, pant* "—don't think—" *pant, pant* "—the mean principal saw me."

"Where were you?" Abby asked.

Lincoln held up an enormous cup from a fast-food place. He sipped through a straw and said, "You guys have better drinks than we do."

I just love the fizz!

SLURP

SLURP

"They're looking for you in Springfield," Doc said.

"Never mind Springfield," Lincoln said. "That fake Lincoln was right!"

He lifted his hat and pulled out a folded piece of paper. It was a poster for the wrestling tournament at the school that night.

"I had no idea it was possible to earn a living as a wrestler," Lincoln said. "This is my big chance—don't you see?"

"Not at all," Doc said.

"I can meet these wonderful athletes, find out how it all works. Find out how I can try out myself!"

"Wait," Abby said. "Try out for what?"

"To be a professional wrestler!" Lincoln practically roared. "Far more fun than sitting around in my living room. And you and your friends will finally care about me!"

"What about history?" Doc asked.

"What about it?"

"History needs you," Abby said. "We all need you."

"Too late for that now," Lincoln said. "You two *did* try, I'll give you that. It didn't work out. And to be honest, I'm not sorry, far from it! I feel free from the stress and worry of my usual responsibilities! Free to get into the ring and wrestle!" Lincoln put his ear to the door. "Voices. The coast isn't clear! Never mind, I'll go out the window!"

And he did.

CHAPTER THIRTEEN

Doc paced back and forth. Abby rested her chin in her hands.

Five minutes passed.

"Any great ideas?" Doc asked.

"Not yet," Abby said.

Through the door, they could hear Ms. Ventura and Mr. Biddle talking and laughing.

"What're *they* laughing about?" Doc said. "This is all their fault!"

Doc flung the door open.

Mr. Biddle was handing Ms. Ventura books from a little cart, and she was shelving them. The gym teacher was still in his Lincoln outfit, but with the beard dangling on his chest like a hairy bow tie.

"Thanks for nothing, Abe!" Doc shouted.

Mr. Biddle looked over. "Huh?"

"And you, too, Ms. Ventura, with your very special guest," Doc said, making air quotes around the last three words. "Now the real Abraham Lincoln is quitting history to become a pro wrestler. I hope you're happy!"

"What on earth is he talking about?" Ms. Ventura asked.

"Sorry, Doc," Mr. Biddle said. "I can't help it if I'm a better Lincoln than that guy."

"That's a lie!" Doc said. "Right, Abby?"

But Abby had stopped listening. Her eyes were huge. If lightbulbs really appeared above people's heads when they had great ideas, you'd have seen one up there.

(NOT REAL, BUT YOU GET THE POINT.)

I've got it!

"You okay?" Doc asked.

Abby nodded. She walked up to Doc and whispered in his ear. "Mr. Biddle thinks he's such a great Abraham Lincoln. Let's let him prove it."

"How?" Doc asked.

"You know," she said. "The cardboard box."

"I don't get—" he started to say. But then he said, "Ohhhhhhhhh. Clever."

And then he said, "Mr. Biddle, could you come in here? We just found something really cool."

Mr. Biddle walked into the storage room. "What's up, guys?"

"It's, um, it's this big box," Doc said.

"What about it?"

Abby pushed a chair up against the side of the cardboard box.

"It's just . . ." she started. "We found something really interesting in there."

"Yeah," Doc said. "Dodgeballs."

"Dodgeballs?" Mr. Biddle asked.

"Tons of them," Doc said.

"Those should be in the gym," Mr. Biddle said. "Let me see."

He stepped onto the chair and opened the flaps of the box. He leaned over to look in. "I don't see any dodgeballs. It's just a bunch of— hey, let go of me!"

"Sorry!" Doc yelled.

And he and Abby lifted the gym teacher's legs off the chair.

"Seriously, guys, I'm gonna fall in!"

"It's for a good cause!" Abby yelled.

Grunting with effort, they lifted Mr. Biddle higher. He tilted forward and fell, screaming, into the box.

YAAAAH!

Then the room went quiet.

"I better go with him," Doc said.

Abby agreed. "Just make sure he messes up history."

"Shouldn't be hard."

"And I'll make sure Lincoln sees it."

"Think that'll get him to go back?" Doc asked.

"Worth a try," Abby said.

"Okay. Good luck."

"Good luck."

Doc stepped onto the chair and dove into the box.

CHAPTER FOURTEEN

Abby raced through the library and down the hall to the cafeteria, which was also the gym. The lunch tables were gone, and in the middle of the room was a wrestling ring. Teachers and parent volunteers were setting up folding chairs. The smell of fresh popcorn floated out from the kitchen.

Abby looked around the big room. *Think, Abby. Think.*

On one side of the room was a stage, where they did concerts and plays. And sometimes they pulled down a screen and showed movies.

The screen! That's it!

No one noticed as Abby climbed onto the stage and dashed into the corner where there was a laptop on a cart. She was pretty sure the computer was hooked up to the screen.

Abby opened the laptop and logged in using her mom's password. She went online and searched for history shows about Lincoln. She found a website that had the exact same show she'd seen with her father the night before. She clicked Play and watched a little bit of it.

The screen showed a photo of a busy street in Springfield, Illinois.

The narrator was saying: "Election Day was finally here. All day, and into the evening, people streamed into Springfield to vote. Yet Abraham Lincoln was still missing. No one had seen—oh, wait, there he is."

And the screen showed the outside of the Lincoln home. Mr. Biddle, with his beard still hanging loose, walked up the steps toward the front door. Doc was right beside him.

"Lincoln finally returned home," the narrator said. "But who is that child?"

Abby smiled. "Nice work, Doc," she said. She stopped the show.

All she'd have to do now was wait for just the right time to lower the screen and press Play.

"Another biscuit?" Mary Lincoln asked, holding out a tray.

"Thanks," Doc said, taking a few.

Doc, Mary Lincoln, and Mr. Biddle were sitting in the parlor of the Lincoln home, having tea. Mrs. Lincoln held the plate of biscuits toward the gym teacher.

Mr. Biddle said. "What's going on here? Where are we?"

Mary smiled. Yes, she was well aware that this man was not her husband. She could guess what Doc was up to and was doing her best to play along.

"Mr. Lincoln is a bit nervous, and understandably so," Mary said to Doc. "There is a very good chance he will be elected president today."

Doc looked out the window. It was getting dark, and the party was starting. Booming brass bands rolled by on wagons. Crowds were marching through the streets, holding torches, talking and shouting.

Mary checked the clock. "We're to meet our friends and supporters in town. And if you win, Mr. Lincoln, you'll be expected to say a few words to the crowd."

Mr. Biddle said, "What about the wrestling?"

"Excuse me?" Mary asked.

"I don't want to miss the wrestling," Mr. Biddle said.

"Come on, you'll be great," Doc said. "You did such a good job as Lincoln today. People loved you!"

Mr. Biddle smiled. "They did, didn't they?"

"Just do more of that kind of stuff," Doc said.

Mary Lincoln stood up. "We'd best be going. Mr. Lincoln, would you please fix your beard?"

Mr. Biddle hooked the beard around his ears. He walked to the front door with Doc and Mrs. Lincoln.

The moment they stepped outside, the crowd in the street gave a huge cheer.

CHAPTER FIFTEEN

The crowd in the school gym gave a huge cheer.

In the wrestling ring, Gigantic Phil climbed onto the ropes and lifted his arms in air. His opponent, Al "The Alligator" Albertson, was lying facedown on the mat.

Prepare to feel the thunder!

"Now he's going to jump on that poor fellow?" Lincoln asked Abby. They were sitting together a few rows from the ring.

"Of course," Abby said. "That's his big move."

"But the man is injured!"

"It's all fake," Abby said. "They plan it out ahead of time."

"This is not the kind of wrestling I'm used to," Lincoln said.

Gigantic Phil leaped from the top rope, soared through the air, and slammed his elbow into the back of The Alligator's head.

GRAAAAAAH!

Or, it looked as if he did. Really, he missed by a few inches. Everyone but Lincoln knew this.

The Alligator rolled around in fake agony. Gigantic Phil dragged his opponent to the edge of the ring. He ducked between the ropes, jumped to the floor, grabbed The Alligator by his feet, and yanked him out of the ring and onto the gym floor.

Kids and adults leaped to their feet and roared.

"Stop the fight!" Lincoln shouted. "Someone stop it!"

No one heard him. The crowd was going crazy.

Gigantic Phil motioned for a girl in the front row to stand up. She did, and he grabbed her chair. He folded the chair and raised it high above The Alligator, who lay on the floor, holding up his hands, pleading, "No! Please!"

"This is too much!" Lincoln screamed. "Put that chair down, sir!"

He started pushing his way toward the ring.

Gigantic Phil looked to the crowd, grinning like a villain.

"Do it!" people shouted.

"Hit him!"

And he was about to. He started swinging—but Abraham Lincoln gripped a leg of the chair and yanked it from Gigantic Phil's grasp.

Phil turned toward Lincoln.

"What are you doing?" Phil demanded.

"Can't you see that man is beaten?" Lincoln asked.

"Yeah, so?"

"So this is no longer a fair fight," Lincoln said.

Gigantic Phil and Abraham Lincoln glared at each other.

The crowd was loving it—they thought this was all part of the show.

"It's that Lincoln guy from school!"
someone shouted.

"Hit him, Phil!" people shouted.

"Go, Lincoln!"

"Go, Phil!"

"You want a fair fight?" Lincoln asked. "I
will give you a fair fight!"

Abraham Lincoln climbed into the wrestling ring.

Gigantic Phil put down the folding chair. He looked around, waiting for someone to tell him what was happening.

Lincoln took off his hat and jacket. He started rolling up his sleeves.

———•———

In Springfield, a man stepped out of the telegraph office and held a piece of paper above his head.

"The results from the East are in!" he shouted.

The street went silent.

"Lincoln has won in Pennsylvania and New York!" the man bellowed. "Our own Abraham Lincoln will be the next president of the United States!"

The crowd roared, waving torches.

Doc and Mary nodded to each other. Doc

guided Mr. Biddle to the front of the crowd.

"Here he is, folks!" Doc said. "Abraham Lincoln!"

People shouted:

"Our own Honest Abe!"

"Mr. President!"

The gym teacher stood on the sidewalk, looking out at hundreds of happy faces.

They were waiting for him to say something.

Anything.

"Um, okay, yeah," Mr. Biddle said.

Anything but that.

"Tell us about your plans as president!" someone shouted.

"Right, plans . . ." Mr. Biddle said. "I have a lot of them. Big plans. Small plans. All kinds of plans."

"Like what?"

"Hey, check this out," Mr. Biddle said, flexing his arms. "You don't get pipes like that from playing video games!"

Everyone stared.

"Guys, look," he said, "I'm definitely going to say some wise things. But first, let's get that blood flowing. Who knows how to do jumping jacks?"

No one did.

CHAPTER SIXTEEN

Gigantic Phil and Abraham Lincoln slowly circled each other in the ring.

Lincoln leaned forward, reaching out his long arms. He grabbed for Gigantic Phil, but Phil hopped out of the way.

They circled each other again.

Gigantic Phil lowered his head like a ram and charged. He hugged Lincoln around the waist, trying to twist him to the ground. Lincoln staggered but would not go down.

Lincoln broke free and backed away. Then he darted forward, seized the sides of Gigantic Phil's tiny shorts, and lifted the large man off the mat. The crowd gasped in shock as Lincoln flipped Gigantic Phil up onto his shoulders.

"Take it easy, bud," Phil said. "This is just for fun."

"I'm having tremendous fun!" Lincoln shouted.

Gigantic Phil started swinging wildly but couldn't grab hold of any part of Lincoln. Lincoln twirled around and around, spinning Phil like a helicopter blade.

Phil finally broke free and dropped six feet, crashing hard onto the mat. He was dizzy. And mad.

He grabbed Lincoln's legs and lifted, sending Lincoln tumbling. As Abe tried to get up, Phil grabbed his arm and tossed him across the ring. Lincoln flew into the ropes, bounced off, and stumbled back toward Phil. Phil drove his shoulder into Abe, knocking him flat on his back.

BONK!

Lincoln sat up, his head spinning.

"Perhaps I'm too old for this," he said.

The crowd went wild when they saw Gigantic Phil climb onto the ropes.

Abby was the only one who noticed a short woman in a long dress make her way toward the wrestling ring.

Just as Gigantic Phil was about to leap, Mary Lincoln climbed into the ring. Phil stopped himself, balanced on the top rope, looking down.

Mrs. Lincoln looked from Phil to her husband and back to Phil.

She said, "What do you boys think you're doing?"

Abby got up and ran to the stage.

———————•———————

"One hundred and four!" Mr. Biddle counted. "One hundred and five! One hundred and six!"

Doc watched from the sidewalk in front of the telegraph office. Things could hardly be going any better.

Mr. Biddle's beard had come loose again, and it was bouncing up and down and hitting him in the nose. "Come on, guys!" he shouted, "Do 'em with me!"

A few people tried doing jumping jacks, but they were packed too tightly, and their flying arms banged together. So they stopped.

Someone in the crowd yelled out: "The leaders of many Southern states have vowed to leave the Union if you won. What do you say to them?"

Mr. Biddle stopped.

"The whole country could start breaking apart before you even get to Washington," another person shouted. "What will you do about that?"

"Um, I, well . . ." Mr. Biddle said. "Did you know I was born in a log cabin? Dirt floor and everything."

The crowd was getting impatient.

"We know about the log cabin!"

"We want to know what you'll do as president!"

"Can you save the Union?"

"Who here knows how to do squat thrusts?" Mr. Biddle asked. "Such a great full-body workout. Watch and learn!"

———•———

In the school gym, the movie screen above the stage began to lower.

Abby was sitting at the computer. The website with the Lincoln history show was still open.

But no one noticed her or the screen.

They were all staring at the woman who had interrupted the wrestling match.

"Time to come home, Mr. Lincoln," Mary said. "Can you stand?"

"I think so," he said.

He groaned as he pushed himself up.

"Now, Mr. Lincoln, while you've been busy with this nonsense, you might be interested to know that the people have just elected you president of the United States."

"That's not my concern," Lincoln said. "I have a new career now."

"He's pretty good," Gigantic Phil said, jumping down from the ropes.

"Pleased to meet you," Mary said. She shook Phil's hand, then turned to her husband. "Are you ready to go?"

"Sorry, no," Abe said. "My mind's made up."

Abby hit Play on the history show. She turned the volume all the way up.

CHAPTER SEVENTEEN

Everyone in the gym looked up at the show on the screen.

They saw Mr. Biddle attempting to teach the people of Springfield about squat thrusts.

"But no one was squatting in Springfield," said the narrator of the show. "No one was thrusting. A lot of people were starting to walk away, grumbling as they headed home."

"Well, Lincoln has always been a bit odd," one man said.

"Sure, but tonight he really cracked," another guy said.

"Must be the pressure of becoming president at a time like this."

"Oh, well. There goes the country."

"Come back!" Mr. Biddle shouted. "I know they're hard! That's why they're good for you!"

Abraham Lincoln stood in the wrestling ring, a look of horror on his face.

"That's not how it's supposed to happen," Lincoln said.

"And are you just going to let that happen?" Mary Lincoln asked.

"Well, I—" Lincoln noticed Abby on the stage. "This was all *your* doing, I suppose."

"And Doc," Abby said. "You can thank

us later." Walking to the front of the stage, she shouted, "You see what would happen without Abraham Lincoln? We really do need Lincoln! The real one!"

"That's nice of you," Lincoln said. "But I don't know . . ."

"What do you guys say?" Abby asked the crowd. "Who thinks Abraham Lincoln would make a good president?"

"Better president than wrestler!" someone shouted.

The crowd laughed.

"You may be right, sir," Lincoln said, rubbing his lower back.

"A lot of you guys saw him in school today," Abby said. "He's great, right? Awesome stories and jokes! Okay, forget the jokes, but we were totally wrong to call him boring. It's not just that he did important stuff—that's true—but the thing is, he's actually a fun guy to hang around with!"

"Thank you, Abby," Lincoln said. "That means a lot to me."

Abby smiled at Lincoln, then turned back to the crowd. "And we're going to pay attention to him from now on, right? We want to see what he does next!"

The students cheered.

"That's all I ever asked," Lincoln said.

He looked up to the screen. Mr. Biddle was being interviewed by a newspaper editor.

The editor asked, "Do you think there is any way to prevent war between the North and the South?"

"I certainly do," Mr. Biddle said.

"And how can that be done?"

"Simple," said Mr. Biddle. "We'll settle our differences with one giant game of dodgeball."

Abraham Lincoln took his wife's arm. "Let's go, Mrs. Lincoln," he said. "We have work to do."

"People here aren't very nice," Mr. Biddle said.

"I guess not," Doc said.

He and Mr. Biddle were walking down a dark street in Springfield.

"Why were they getting so angry at me?" Mr. Biddle asked.

Doc wasn't sure how to explain.

They were almost back to the Lincoln house when Doc heard Abby's voice.

"Doc! There you are!"

Abby ran up. Abraham and Mary Lincoln were right behind her.

"You're back!" Doc said to Abe.

"I'm back," he said.

"Yes, thanks to the two of you," Mary said to Doc and Abby.

"You might want to go down there," Doc said to Abe, pointing toward the center of town. "People really want to hear from you. The real you, I mean."

"Of course, right away," Lincoln said. "But I want to thank you for all that you've done."

"The whole school-visit idea didn't go exactly as planned," Abby said.

Lincoln laughed. "Perhaps not."

"But we did it," Doc said. "We fixed history!"

"I wouldn't go that far," Lincoln said.

Doc and Abby looked at him, surprised.

"But you're back," Abby said. "You're going to be president."

"I am, I am. But, you see . . . I can't speak for the others."

"Others?"

Lincoln seemed a little embarrassed. "It's my fault as much as yours," he said. "I was trying to teach you a lesson. And it worked, I suppose . . . but, they all saw. They don't have to do the same old thing anymore. They realize that now."

"They?" Abby asked. "You mean other historical characters?"

"We're not characters, we're *people*," Lincoln said. "What I'm saying is that history might start to get a little mixed up. If Abigail Adams wants to become, oh, I don't know, a pirate—what's to stop her?"

"Who's Abigail Adams?" Doc asked.

"I'll pretend I didn't hear that," Lincoln said. "But *she* did, you can bet. Look, I'm going to talk to them, all of them. I'll do my best to keep things moving along as they should. But I can't promise anything. You're going to want to keep an eye on that history book of yours."

"We will," Abby said.

"And can I count on you?" Lincoln asked. "If I need your help to set things right?"

"Anytime," Doc said. "You know where to find us."

"Good."

Lincoln shook hands with Abby and Doc.

It's been
an honor.

Then he said to Mr. Biddle, "If you hurry,
you can catch the last few wrestling matches."

CHAPTER EIGHTEEN

Abby, Doc, and Mr. Biddle watched Abraham and Mary Lincoln walk away. Moments later, a huge cheer erupted in the center of town.

Abby and Doc smiled at each other. Their work was done.

"So," Mr. Biddle said, "how do we get out of here?"

"That's a good question," Doc said.

"You mean you don't know?"

"Well, we've done it before," Abby said.

"So do it again," Mr. Biddle said.

"But we don't know how," Abby said. "Last time, it sort of just happened."

"That's not exactly right," Doc said.

"What do you mean?"

"We were talking with Lincoln, remember?" Doc said. "And I was telling him how all the kids in our class think history is . . . I don't know if I can say it."

"Say what?" Abby asked.

"I don't want Lincoln to hear," Doc said. "Or that Adams lady, whoever she is."

He looked toward town.

"Just try it," Abby said.

"But I don't believe it anymore," Doc said.

"Just say it," Abby said.

Doc looked around. No one was watching. He said, very quietly, "History is boring."

And they were gone.

———•———

The big cardboard box in the library storage room rocked back and forth and tipped over. The top flaps opened and Abby, Doc, and Mr. Biddle crawled out.

Mr. Biddle stood up and looked around.

"I should probably report this whole thing
to Principal Darling," he said. "Tell her that you
guys pushed me into this box and then, well . . ."

He was about to say more—but he was

stopped by a huge burst of shouts and claps from the crowd in the gym.

"The wrestling!" Mr. Biddle shouted. "I'm not too late!"

He ran out the door. Doc and Abby got up.

"So . . ." Abby said.

"Yeah," Doc said.

They set the box upright.

"We better find Mom," Abby said. "She was asking where you've been."

"What should we tell her?" Doc asked.

"I don't know. Studying history?"

Doc laughed. "She'll never believe it."

"I know. Fixing history?"

"But did we?" Doc asked. "I can't tell if we fixed history or broke it."

"I guess we'll find out," Abby said.

"Guess so."

Doc turned off the light as they left the storage room. Abby made sure to shut the door behind them.

The room was quiet and dark. A streetlamp in the parking lot cast a faint yellow glow on the tall cardboard box.

———•———

Ten hours later, the sun began to rise. The library storage room slowly filled with light.

The cardboard box began to shake.

UN-TWISTING HISTORY

So, aside from the stuff I obviously made up—like Lincoln suddenly popping out of a cardboard box—how much of this book is based on real history?

A lot of it, actually. Abraham Lincoln really was born in a log cabin in Kentucky, and he really was so busy working on his family's

farm that he hardly ever went to school. And it's true that he loved to read. "The things I want to know are in books," twelve-year-old Abe once said. "My best friend is the man who'll get me a book I ain't read."

As Lincoln told the kids in the school library, he didn't get along with his father and left home to work on a riverboat on the Mississippi. This is where he saw enslaved African Americans for the first time and began thinking about how cruel and evil slavery was.

Settling in Illinois, he found work as a clerk in a general store. Once, realizing a customer had paid too much for something, Lincoln walked four miles to return the woman's change. That's when people started calling him "Honest Abe"—a nickname he hated, apparently.

He became a lawyer and, at the age of twenty-three, ran for a seat in the Illinois state legislature. He came in eighth. It was not the last election he'd lose. After losing a race for the US Senate in 1858, he told friends, "I feel just like a boy who stubbed his toe—too badly hurt to laugh, and too proud to cry."

That's classic Lincoln—he had a joke for every situation. As president, he was famous for starting meetings with funny stories, puns, or riddles. This annoyed some people, but it was Lincoln's way of dealing with the incredible stress of his job. The jokes I included in this book are all jokes Lincoln really told.

If you didn't think they were very funny, you're not alone. Mary Lincoln was not a fan of her husband's gags.

Lincoln really did love to play handball in an alley near his law office in Springfield, and yes, his horse truly was named Old Bob. Anyone who's seen photos of Lincoln knows he really did wear a tall, stovepipe hat. At six-foot-four, he's the tallest president in American history, so he already stood out in a crowd. But he liked *really* standing out, which is part of the reason he wore the tall hat. Also, he really did keep papers and notes in the lining of his hat. The kids of Springfield knew this and had fun figuring out ways to knock Lincoln's hat off.

The beard story is totally true. Historians have found the full text of Grace Bedell's letter to Lincoln in which she suggests the beard, and there are newspaper stories about Lincoln meeting Grace on his way to Washington, DC.

Who came up with the design of Lincoln's distinctive beard? The most likely answer is William de Fleurville, an immigrant from Haiti who owned several businesses, including a barbershop, in Springfield. Fleurville sometimes hired Lincoln to do legal work, and Lincoln went to Fleurville's shop for shaves and haircuts. They were friends for over twenty years. So when Lincoln decided to start growing a beard, it's only logical that Fleurville would have been involved.

WILLIAM DE FLEURVILLE

In the scene with Abby and Doc in the family living room, Mr. Douglass gives a very quick summary of the Civil War. This was by far the deadliest war in American history and way too big and complicated to explain here. I'm hoping you'll be curious enough to find out more. Anyway, just to finish the story . . . Lincoln was reelected in 1864. In April 1865, the United States finally defeated the Confederacy. More than six hundred thousand soldiers had died in the Civil War. The Thirteenth Amendment to the Constitution banned slavery in the United States.

On the evening of April 14, 1865, Abraham and Mary Lincoln went to a play at Ford's Theatre in Washington. During the show, an actor named John Wilkes Booth, who was bitter about the South's defeat, sneaked up behind Lincoln and shot him. Abraham Lincoln died early the next morning.

His body was taken back to Springfield, Illinois, where friends built him a tomb and monument that you can still visit today.

You can—and should—form your own opinions. But I guess you can tell I'm a big Abraham Lincoln fan. I'd argue that he had the hardest job of any president in the history of the United States. When historians rank the best presidents, they usually put Lincoln number one, and I totally agree.

He was also never, ever boring.

Oh, and one more thing. Abraham Lincoln really is in the National Wrestling Hall of Fame.

Look it up.

OH NO! ABRAHAM LINCOLN WAS RIGHT. FAMOUS FOLKS FROM HISTORY KNOW THEY DON'T HAVE TO DO THE SAME OLD THING ANYMORE—AND EVERYTHING IS TWISTING OUT OF CONTROL!

FIND OUT WHAT HAPPENS IN THE NEXT TIME TWISTERS ADVENTURE:

AVAILABLE NOW!

CREDITS

STEVE SHEINKIN, *Author*

NEIL SWAAB, *Illustrator / Designer*

CONNIE HSU, *Executive Editor*

SIMON BOUGHTON, *Publisher*

ELIZABETH CLARK, *Art Director*

TOM NAU, *Director of Production*

JILL FRESHNEY, *Senior Executive Managing Editor*

MEGAN ABBATE, *Editorial Assistant*

OH NO! NOW FAMOUS FOLKS FROM HISTORY
KNOW THEY DON'T HAVE TO DO THE SAME
OLD THING ANYMORE—AND EVERYTHING IS
TWISTING OUT OF CONTROL!

FIND OUT WHAT HAPPENS IN THE NEXT
TIME TWISTERS ADVENTURE.

COMING FALL 2018!